For Cliff—who would give me the shirt off his back
—CRS

For Daniel—who warms me when I'm c-c-cold
—KC

For Cathy
—CO

ABOUT THIS BOOK

The illustrations for this book were done in pencil, scanned textures, and digital paint. This book was edited by Deirdre Jones and designed by Véronique Lefèvre Sweet. The production was supervised by Patricia Alvarado, and the production editor was Marisa Finkelstein. The text was set in Grandma Bold, the title type is set in the author's hand lettering, and the display type is Hen House AOE Regular.

Cold Turkey

By Corey Rosen Schwartz & Kirsti Call

Illustrated by Chad Otis

L B

Little, Brown and Company

New York   Boston

Turkey woke up c-c-cold.
He wheezed, "It's ten degrees!

I need to b-b-bundle up
before I f-f-freeze!"

COLD TURKEY

Sheep was sh-sh-shivering.
Her shoulders sh-sh-shook.

"I can't baa-lieve this storm's so baad.
I need a warmer nook."

SHIVERING SHEEP

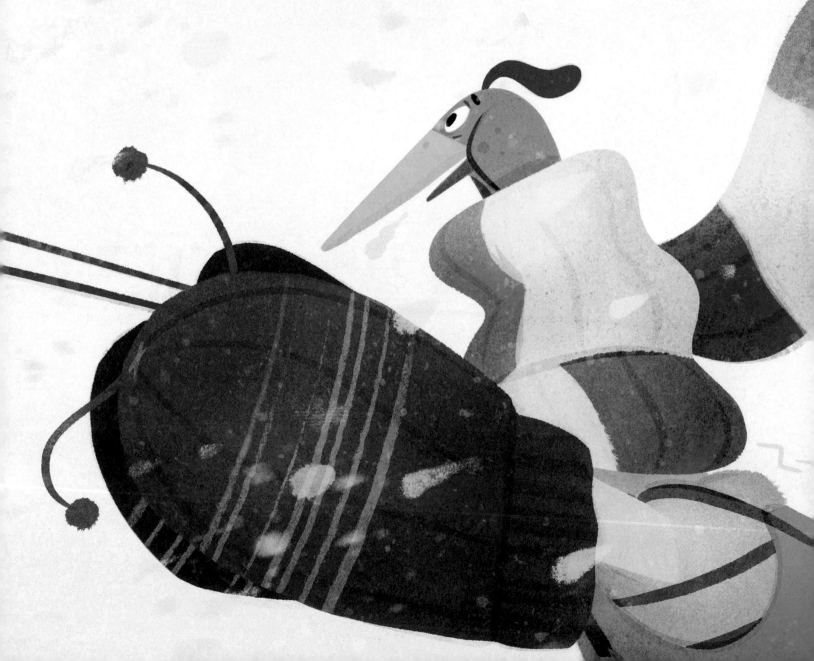

Chick was fl-fl-fluttering,
cooped up and all alone.

"My beak is ch-ch-chattering.
I'm chilled right to the bone."

Horse was h-h-huddling
beneath a heap of hay.

"I'm frozen through. My lips are blue.
It's hard to n-n-neigh!"

HUDDLING
HORSE

Cow was qu-qu-quivering.
"I can't help but complain.

This wind is a cow-tastrophy!
It's udderly insane."

QUIVERING COW

Pig was p-p-poking out
from p-p-piles of straw.

"My body's numb, from snout to bum.
I don't know when I'll thaw."

POLAR PIG

Turkey tr-tr-trembled.
He had loaned out all his loot.
He wobbled homeward, cold and bare,
in just his birthday suit!

Turkey t-t-tottered.
"What a fierce, ferocious storm!
I may be getting frostbite,
but at least my heart feels warm."

The barnyard gang felt grateful
so they built their friend a fire.

They gathered c-c-close until…